OLIVIA™
and the Haunted Hotel

adapted by Jodie Shepherd
based on the screenplay
"OLIVIA Plays Hotel"
written by Kate Boutilier and
Eryk Casemiro

illustrated by Patrick Spaziante

Simon Spotlight
New York   London   Toronto   Sydney

Based on the TV series *OLIVIA*™ as seen on Nickelodeon®

SIMON SPOTLIGHT
An imprint of Simon & Schuster Children's Publishing Division
1230 Avenue of the Americas, New York, New York 10020
Copyright © 2010 Silver Lining Productions Limited (a Chorion company).
All rights reserved. OLIVIA™ and © 2010 Ian Falconer. All rights reserved.
All rights reserved, including the right of reproduction in whole or in part in any form.
SIMON SPOTLIGHT and colophon are registered trademarks of Simon & Schuster, Inc.
For information about special discounts for bulk purchases, please contact Simon & Schuster Special Sales
at 1-866-506-1949 or business@simonandschuster.com.
Manufactured in the United States of America 0710 LAK   First Edition   1 2 3 4 5 6 7 8 9 10
ISBN 978-1-4424-0182-2

"Look at all that rain!" exclaimed Olivia. "Thunder and lightning, too. I love spooky weather!"

"Did you have fun at school today?" asked Mother.
Before anyone could answer there was an enormous *BOOM* of thunder.
Ian and Olivia yelled, "Wooohoo!"

"I know the perfect game to play when we get to my house," said Olivia.

"Welcome to the Hotel Olivia," Olivia greets her guests.

"Please come in and make yourselves at home."

"Wow, it's so big!" Francine says.

"This is nothing," answers Olivia. "You should see my other hotels."

Olivia's house made a perfect hotel.

"I'd like a room, please," Francine requested.

"Me too," said Julian. "I mean a different room. Maybe one with a TV."

"Of course," Olivia replied politely. "That shouldn't be a problem."

There was a flash of lightning. *Whooo! Tap, tap, tap.*

The wind whistled and tree branches tapped on the windowpanes.

"What was that sound?" asked Julian nervously.

"Sounds like a ghost," Francine said, trembling.

"Ghost? The Hotel Olivia has no ghosts," Olivia answered firmly.

"Follow me, please."

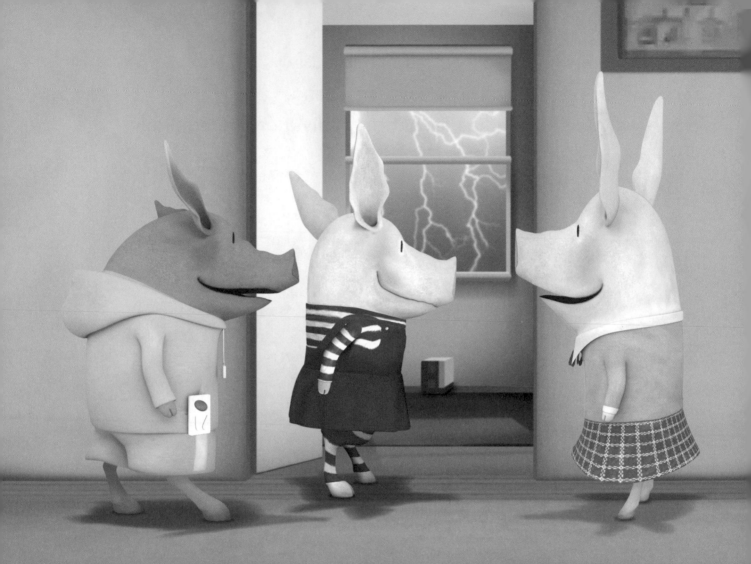

"This is your room, Francine," said Olivia, opening a door.

"No offense, Olivia," said Francine, "but I'd like another room. This one smells like boy."

"I'll take it," said Julian. "I already smell like boy. Does it come with room service?"

"Of course," Olivia answered, opening the door to a second room. "All our rooms do. They also come with fluffy towels and chocolates on the pillows. That's what makes the Hotel Olivia the fanciest hotel in the world."

"I love my new room!" cried Francine. "This is the best hotel ever!"

Brring! A bell rang from downstairs.

"Excuse me," said Olivia. "I think I have another customer."

"I'm sorry, but the Hotel Olivia is completely full," Olivia told Ian.
"No fair," complained Ian. "Mom! Olivia says all the rooms in her hotel are taken."
"Olivia, I'm sure you can find a room for Ian *somewhere* in your large hotel," said Mother.

"This is our last room," Olivia announced. "You'll love the privacy.
Plus the soaps are free. But you'll have to leave when the other guests
need to use the bathroom."

"Never mind. I don't want to stay at this hotel anyway," said Ian.

"Besides, I heard there were ghosts."

"Ghosts!" repeated Francine and Julian.

Room service kept Olivia very busy—too busy to play with her brother. She delivered lunches,

made beds,

cleaned up dog toys,

and soothed frightened guests.
"It's just the hotel laundry," reassured
Olivia.

That gave Ian an idea.

Suddenly there was a loud bang and everything went dark.

"HEY! WHO TURNED OUT THE LIGHTS?" yelled Francine, alarmed.

"The storm must have knocked the power out," guessed Julian.

"Or a ghost did," whispered Francine.
"I told you, Francine," said Olivia, "there are no ghosts at this hotel."

"BOO!"
"Aah! Ghost!" screamed Francine.
"Aah! I see it too!" screamed Julian.
"Where? There are no ghosts at the Hotel Olivia,"
Olivia repeated.

Francine and Julian huddled together. "Well, I saw a ghost," said Francine, "and I don't want to stay in this spooky hotel anymore." "Me neither," Julian agreed. "This hotel is haunted."

HMM. If I do have a ghost in my hotel, then I'm just going to have to get rid of it, Olivia thinks. Good thing I have a Ghost-o-Meter.

"I *knew* it was you, Ian!" said Olivia. Then she called downstairs.
"Mom, Ian is scaring my guests."
"Well, Olivia, maybe Ian just wants to play," Mother called back.
"Hmm," said Olivia. "I know! Ian, how would you like to be the room-service waiter?"
"Cool!" said Ian.

"Welcome to breakfast at the ghost-free Hotel Olivia," said Ian the next morning. "Today we are serving our world-famous pancakes."

"Yum," said Francine.

"Double yum," said Julian.

"More pancakes, anyone?" asked Mother.